WEREWOLF MAX

AND THE MIDNIGHT ZOMBIES

BOOK 1

N. A

ISBN: 978-1-7338595-1-6

www.nadavenport.com

Library of Congress Control Number: 2019904740

❀ Created with Vellum

Contents

ONE

The Attack

IT WAS cold the night Max got bit. The icy February air made his breath look like smoke. His nose and ears stung in the wind. Max shoved his hands under his arms to keep his fingers warm.

He was on his way home from his friend Tim's house. Even though they had different fourth grade teachers, he and Tim still spent most afternoons together. But today they'd been so busy playing video games that they didn't notice the time until it was already late. Now it was dark out and his mom was going to be mad. Max was old enough to walk home alone, he did it all the time, but he was supposed to be back when the street lights turned on.

He looked up. The lights shone orange over his

head. The full moon rose into the sky above them. It cast a pale light onto the street below.

Suddenly, Max heard a howl. It was a deep sound, loud and wild, and it came from somewhere close by. He stopped walking to look around.

A pair of red eyes stared at him from the darkness under the trees.

The creature howled again. The sound made Max tremble.

He turned and raced up the hill toward home as fast as he could. His heart pounded in his chest. The cold air burned in his lungs. He could hear the monster running behind him. Its claws scraped in the dirt. Its heavy paws thumped on the ground. Its breathing was loud and deep.

Something hit him. Hard.

Max fell to the ground and his face smashed into the dirt. Something heavy and hairy held him down. He felt hot breath in his ear as its claws dug into his coat. He smelled the doggy stink of fur.

Then it bit down on his arm. Sharp teeth pierced through his coat and into his skin.

Max cried out in pain as warm blood wet his sleeve. The monster pulled at him with its teeth. It was going to eat him!

Just then a car drove up the road, its headlights shining. The driver honked his horn and the blaring noise hurt Max's ears. At the sound, the creature let go, whined, and ran away into the woods.

Max sat up, crying, and wiped the dirt from his face.

The car door opened and a man stepped out. "Are you okay there?" the driver asked. "That was the biggest dog I ever saw!"

Max's arm hurt where the thing had bit him. He was still bleeding. He pressed his hand over the wound in pain. Dirt and grass still clung to his face.

The man walked closer, looked at Max's arm, and

frowned. "Ouch! Looks like you got a nasty bite there. I'll walk you home. Where do you live?"

Max was still crying. His arm hurt badly. When he finally was able to say where his house was, the man walked him the remaining block home.

"Where have you been? I was so worried!" Max's mom yelled when he got to the door.

"I saw a dog attack him out by the park," the man said. "Biggest dog I ever saw. He got a bite on his arm. You might want to take a look at it."

Max's mom looked at his arm and gasped at the blood. Her eyes widened. "Oh, thank you! Thank you for bringing him home!"

"No problem," the man said. He nodded and walked back down the street to his car.

Max's mom took him to the bathroom where she pulled off his coat and shirt. The bite on his arm looked like rows of deep red holes. Blood smeared across his skin like red paint.

"A dog did this?" she asked.

"I don't know," Max said. "I didn't see it. It was big and hairy."

His mom opened their first-aid kit and started to clean the blood off.

"This looks pretty bad. I think you should see the doctor."

Max nodded but didn't say anything. He knew the man who helped him thought it was a dog. But dogs didn't howl like that. Dogs weren't that big. Dogs didn't have glowing red eyes. Max knew the truth. What bit him was some kind of monster.

TWO

Not a Dog Bite

"Hmm…" The doctor frowned. He touched the bite marks with his gloved hand. It hurt, and Max jerked away.

"Sorry, please hold still."

Max tried to be still while the doctor cleaned his arm. The wet cotton stung in his open wounds.

"You should have come sooner," the doctor said. "This could get infected, you know."

"What?" his mom asked. "We came right away. The dog bit him only an hour ago."

The doctor looked up at her. "These wounds look old," he said. "They're already healing."

Max's mom frowned. She looked confused, but she didn't say anything.

The doctor smeared medicine on the bite and

wrapped Max's arm in a bandage. Then he gave Max a shot in his upper arm. The shot stung for a few seconds, but that was all.

"You should be fine now," the doctor said. "But if it gets worse, come back and I'll take a look at it again."

On their way home, Max's mom took them to an ice cream shop. They got a banana split to share, with three flavors of ice cream. His mom left the chocolate scoop for Max because it was his favorite.

"My mom used to buy me ice cream when I went to the doctor," she said. "It always made me feel better." She took a bite of vanilla and smiled at him.

"It does help. My arm doesn't hurt at all now." Max smiled back and scooped some chocolate and caramel sauce into his mouth.

"That's good. I still can't believe there's such a dangerous dog loose. I'll have to report it. Did you see what color it was?"

Max shook his head and took another bite. He knew it wasn't really a dog. It was a big, hairy, smelly monster with red eyes. But his mom wouldn't believe that.

When they got home, Max went right to bed.

That night he had a bad dream. In it he was running from a huge black wolf. No matter how fast he ran, the wolf ran faster. It jumped on him and sank its teeth into his arm. It ripped out chunks of his flesh. It tore off his arms and legs. Its teeth dripped with blood. Finally, it opened its mouth and bit off his head.

Max woke up breathing hard, sweaty, and shivering. His heart was pounding.

He climbed out of bed and went to the bathroom. After he flushed the toilet, he thought he should look at the bite on his arm. Carefully, he took off his shirt and peeled up the bandage. When it didn't hurt, he took it all the way off.

Max's eyes went wide. There was blood on the bandage. And there was some dried blood smeared on his skin. But the bite on his arm was gone!

"Wow," he said. He turned his arm. He moved it up and down. He looked at it all over. There wasn't a mark on it. It didn't hurt. It was like he'd never been bitten at all.

THREE

Strange Things

MAX GOT DRESSED and went downstairs for breakfast.

"How does your arm feel?" his mom asked. She poured some milk into his bowl.

"It's better, mom. It doesn't hurt at all."

"That's good. Go on and eat your breakfast." She glanced at the clock. "You have half an hour until the bus comes."

She made bowls of cereal for his little sisters, too. Mia dropped her spoon and just ate with her hands. She smeared soggy cereal around her highchair tray and squished handfuls in her fists. Max's mom didn't seem to care as long as some of it got into Mia's mouth, too.

Maddie kept drinking all her milk and asking Max to pour more into her bowl for her. She was four years old

11

and only ate cereal without a fight if it was colorful or had sugary marshmallows in it.

Max finished his breakfast and went out to the bus stop. His friend, Tim, was already there, sitting on the ground and digging in the dirt with a sharp stick. He looked up when Max got close.

"Did you get in trouble?" Tim asked. He looked worried.

"Not really," Max said. "My mom was a little mad. But she just said she was worried I was out so late."

He almost told Tim about the creature that attacked him. But the bite wound on his arm was already gone. Tim would think he was making it up.

Tim still looked a little worried, but he shrugged. "Oh, cool. Want to come over and play after school?"

"Yeah!"

Max picked up a stick like Tim's and they fought with them like swords. Tim usually beat Max, but today Max won a few times. Maybe Tim just wasn't paying attention. He knocked the stick out of Tim's hand three times before the bus came.

Other weird things happened that morning, too. It seemed like his hearing was much better. He could understand the girls talking in the front of the noisy bus, even though he sat in the back row. He was also stronger and faster than before. Playing outside before school started, he could run faster and climb higher than most of the other kids.

A big rock lay buried in the dirt by the back fence. A lot of kids had tried to pull it out to see what was under it, but no one ever could. When he saw that no adults were looking, Max went to try again.

He dug his fingers into the cold dirt. The ground felt softer than usual. It was easy! He dug under the rock and pulled. It was heavy, but the rock moved. He pulled harder, and the ground cracked around it. He rolled the rock up and a pile of icy dirt came with it.

The rock was huge! It was a lot bigger than he thought it would be. Only the top had been above ground. Now that it was out, he could see that it was almost as big as he was. In the hole left behind, Max saw stringy white roots, the sticky mesh of spider egg sacs, and the twisted tubes of worm holes. A few black beetles skittered out of sight as soon as the light hit them.

"Dude! You got it up?" someone said from behind him. It was Ian, a boy in his class.

"What? He pulled it out?" asked a girl he didn't know. "No way!"

"Look at that hole!"

"That rock is ginormous!"

"Yeah, right! Someone else pulled it out first." Without turning around, Max knew the voice belonged to Dean. He always said nasty stuff like that. "You can't pick that up. It's too heavy. You're not strong enough."

"I did so pull it out. Just now!" Max said.

"Yeah? Prove it!" Dean sneered.

"Fine, I will!" Max grabbed the edge of the rock. Everyone moved in to watch.

Then the bell rang. It was time to line up for class.

FOUR

Full Moon

"HA! YOU GOT LUCKY THIS TIME!" Dean shoved Max's shoulder and Max rolled to the ground.

Dean laughed and walked away to line up with the rest of his class. Most of the other kids followed him.

Tim held out his hand to help Max up. "Did you really pull the rock out by yourself?"

"Yeah. It wasn't even that hard."

"That's cool!" He smiled at Max. "You must be really strong. Don't listen to Dean. He's just a fart-head."

They laughed and went to line up for class.

During PE, Max felt like everything was way too easy for him. Jump rope? Simple. Dodge balls? No problem. Push-ups? He could do push-ups all day. Run around the track? He could run around the track a hundred times and never feel tired.

He could also smell things he couldn't before. When he was outside at recess, he could smell the spicy beef nachos cooking inside for lunch. He smelled the cars driving on the road and the smoke made him wrinkle his nose. He could tell the difference between the sharp scent of cedar trees and the warm smell of hickory or maple. He could even smell the bugs and animals living in the frozen ground.

By the time he was on the bus home, he knew for sure something weird was happening to him. He was stronger and faster. He could smell the tiniest things. He could hear the faintest noises. But weirdest of all, the palm of his hand had started to itch.

When Max got home, his mom asked how his arm was feeling.

"It doesn't hurt. It's fine," he said.

She made him take his shirt off so she could see it. When he did, she looked at both of his arms carefully, like she wasn't sure which one had been hurt.

"Max, there isn't even a bruise. Your arm doesn't have a mark on it!"

"I know. I guess it wasn't as bad as it looked." He shrugged.

His mom looked like she couldn't believe it. But in the end, she just shook her head and mumbled to herself,

"Well, what am I going to do? Take him to the doctor because his arm isn't hurt anymore?"

As the days passed, Max felt new changes happening. When he got mad, he noticed that he had a hard time controlling his emotions. His vision blurred red. His heart pounded. He felt too hot in his body. His skin started to feel prickly all over. Inside, he could feel something growing, like his guts were getting too big for his chest. While he was angry, the feeling didn't scare him at all. He almost wished he could turn into a monster. But later, when he wasn't angry anymore, he wondered what would happen if he did.

One day, Max was extra mad at everything. It started when his mom wouldn't let him eat a second bowl of cereal because he had to save some for his sisters. "Maddie doesn't even like this cereal," he grumbled. Then, his dad told him he couldn't go to Tim's house after school unless he did all his chores first, and that made him even angrier. He stomped up to his room and saw that his sisters had ripped apart his favorite Lego set that he'd been working on all week. It felt like they were all against him.

Later, at school, Miss Diaz made him read in class and he didn't know where they were in the story. Some of the other kids laughed at him. Max was embarrassed so he talked back to his teacher. She sent him to the office, and when the principal asked him what happened, Max couldn't stop himself from raising his voice in reply. He didn't even know what he was mad at anymore.

Then, on the bus ride home, Tim said he couldn't come over to play. But when Max asked why, Tim wouldn't give a reason. Max got mad and yelled at Tim, too. He left the bus stop with both hands tightened into fists.

After dinner, his mom took his temperature and said he had a fever. His dad sent him to bed early. That made him mad, too.

He paced the floor in his room. Outside, the sky was growing dark blue. The wind howled against the house. The sound made Max want to howl, too.

His hand still itched. A red star shape had appeared on his skin where he scratched it all the time. Having an itchy hand made him mad, too. He kicked his toys and growled.

His room felt too hot. Sweat formed on his forehead and the back of his neck. Max opened his window to let the cold air in. It felt nice, so he leaned out to feel the wind on his hot skin.

Then he saw the moon. It glowed big and round above the trees. Its pale light shone on Max's face.

Suddenly, Max wasn't just mad. He was scared, too.

As he stared at the yellow moon, his skin prickled. Then his face got hot, despite the cool wind blowing through his window. The star on

his hand burned and everything looked strangely red. His guts got too big for his chest. Then a monster exploded inside of him, big and dark and hairy.

Max the werewolf jumped out his window. He landed on the grass with a thud and ran into the night.

FIVE

Monster

MAX WAS SCARED. Max was mad. Max couldn't think clearly at all. He ran on four legs between the houses, up the hill, and past the park. His claws dug deep grooves in the dirt. His paws thumped on the ground. He panted like a dog as he ran. Moving his tongue around, he found a set of long, sharp fangs in his mouth.

He raced into the trees. He didn't know why. He was just scared, so he gave in to the urge to run away.

Then Max smelled something new and tasty, and he was suddenly very hungry. He needed to eat, so he turned and followed the new smell.

He ran back to the dirt trail near the park and found what he was looking for. Two people walked side by side on the trail. He could see them. But they did not see him.

They smelled like the tastiest steaks he'd ever dreamed of. Like juicy ribs sizzling on the grill. He started to drool and licked his chops.

But then something big and hairy hit Max, knocking him to the ground.

He yelped.

Teeth bit into his back leg and tail, pulling on him, dragging him backward.

He jerked around, trying to fight. There were three other werewolves on him. Two were bigger than he was. One was small, about his size.

They grabbed him with their teeth and pulled. Their fangs ripped into his legs and tail as they yanked him into the trees. The big one shoved against him with its head. It jumped away when Max tried to bite but then went right back to pushing.

The werewolves dragged and pushed for a long time. They forced him into the woods until they reached a clearing with tall grass. Max saw more werewolves there, but he was too busy fighting to count them.

They dragged him into the middle of the field and then let him go. The werewolves surrounded Max. They walked in a big circle, staring at him. Three of them had his blood on their lips. Max could smell it. They looked like giant wolves with red eyes. But their noses were shorter than real wolves' noses and their front paws were wide and flat, almost like hands.

Max growled, showing his teeth. The hair on his back and tail stood straight up. His big wolf ears pressed flat against his head.

"Take it easy, little one," the biggest werewolf said. He spoke with his mouth like a person would.

Max was too mad and hurt to listen to him. He growled and barked at the big wolf.

"We don't want to hurt you. But we can't let you kill."

Max turned with his head low. He growled at all the werewolves. They just paced around him in a big circle. Their glowing red eyes trailed him as he shifted nervously on his paws.

"Just keep him here. We'll wait all night if we have to," the big wolf said. He was talking to the others.

Max couldn't stay mad forever, not even if he wanted to, not even if he was a werewolf. As the others walked around him, he started to calm down. He stopped growling and laid down in the grass.

His legs and tail had blood on them from being bitten. But the wounds were better already. He started licking at the blood, cleaning it off like a dog would.

The biggest wolf stepped forward then. The others kept walking in a circle around him.

"Are you ready to listen?" the big wolf asked.

Max put his ears back and growled. But he wasn't as mad or as scared as before.

"We are very sorry for what happened to you. It was an accident. But you are one of us now, a part of our pack. You need to know what that means."

SIX

Scary Stories

"My name is Peter," the big wolf said. "I've been a werewolf for over a hundred years. At first, I was a monster. My whole life was like a bad dream I couldn't wake up from. But in time, I learned how to stop killing people and start helping them instead. There are other monsters out there, though. And we need to protect people from them."

Max heard what Peter was telling him. But inside his head, he was still too scared and angry to think about it.

"I know it's not easy now," Peter said. "Soon, you will learn control. Then you can start to fight with us."

Max looked up at Peter and whined. Then he opened his mouth and tried to make words with his strange teeth and lips. "What... monsters?"

"There is a group of banshees in the area. Do you know what those are?"

Max shook his head no.

"They look like women, but they aren't. At night they can kill people just by screaming at them. And they can turn the dead into zombies."

Max didn't know what to think about this. It sounded like a make-believe story. But turning into a werewolf also sounded like a story. And here he was, Max the werewolf.

"Some of us go out every night to look for them. If we find any zombies—" He stared hard and growled, "—we rip them to pieces."

"They taste awful, too," another wolf said. Some of the others laughed. It was weird to hear human laughter coming from big scary-looking werewolves.

Peter glared at them and they went quiet.

"It will take you some time to get a handle on yourself. You need to practice controlling your anger when you aren't a wolf, and then it will be easier."

Max tilted his head. What did Peter mean, controlling himself?

"If you can control your anger when you're a boy, it will be easier to control your anger as a wolf. Being mad or scared makes you dangerous."

Max thought about this. He'd been angry all day

long without knowing why. But now it made sense. It must have been because he was a werewolf.

"Do you have any questions?" Peter asked.

Max thought. Then he tried to form the words with his strange mouth. "Who... bit... me?"

The other wolves stopped walking around him.

The smallest one looked up at him and walked forward. "I'm sorry, Max. I'm really sorry." His voice sounded familiar.

Max looked at the small werewolf. Slowly, he made the words. "Why did you bite me?"

The small wolf looked at the ground. His tail curled under his body. "I lost control. I wanted to join the others. I wanted to fight with them. But I smelled you walking home alone and I couldn't stop myself."

"Max," Peter said. His voice was gentle. "Young werewolves are wild. It takes a long time to learn control." He looked at the smaller wolf and showed his teeth. "Your friend should not have been out alone during a full moon. That is a lesson I hope you learn soon."

"My friend?" he asked. It was starting to get easier to speak with fangs.

The small wolf whined and lowered his head, so his nose touched the ground. "It's me, Max. I'm Tim."

SEVEN

Bright Idea

THE FULL MOON went down in the middle of the night. Without its light, the werewolves could turn back into people again. It took Max a while to figure out how to do it. Peter said that the sun would make it a lot easier, but he should get back home before his mom worried about him.

When the other wolves changed back, he was surprised to see that some of them were ladies. One was an old man. All of them were dressed in warm clothing like they were ready to be outside in the winter.

The night was icy cold. Max was far from home and wearing only his pajamas. He started shivering and his teeth chattered together.

"Here, you can wear this," Peter put his coat on

Max. "Make sure you dress warmly for the next full moon."

As a human, Peter looked like a normal adult. He had brown hair, brown eyes and looked like he might be the same age as Max's dad. He started walking with Max and Tim, taking them home.

"What happens to our clothes when we're wolves?" Max asked.

Peter laughed. "Who knows? I'm just glad we don't rip them up every time we change."

"And what's this mark on my hand?" He showed Peter the red star on his palm.

"That's the mark of the curse. We all have one." He showed his hand to Max. There was a red star on Peter's hand, too. "It won't itch anymore now that you've gone wolf. But it does get darker when there's a full moon. That will help you know the change is coming."

Tim was very quiet. He didn't talk to Max or Peter the whole way back. When they got to Max's house, his bedroom window was still open wide. His curtains fluttered in the breeze.

"Max?" Tim said.

Max looked at him.

"Do you still want to be friends?"

Max thought about it. "Yeah, I still want to be

friends." Then he smiled. "I need you to teach me how to be a good werewolf, right?"

Tim smiled, too. "I'm not a good werewolf. I almost had you for dinner, remember?"

The boys laughed. Peter didn't.

Max gave the coat back to Peter, climbed up the side of his house, and crawled through his window. It was easy. He was so strong now, it wasn't any harder than climbing stairs.

The next day, Max tried to control himself. Peter had told him to practice. And he really didn't want to start eating people.

He still felt angry at a lot of things, but it wasn't as bad as before, maybe because the moon wasn't full, or maybe because now he understood what was happening to him.

That morning, Maddie went into his room and dumped all of his Lego bricks onto the floor. "Get out!" he yelled at her and she started to cry. But when his face got hot, he stopped and closed his eyes until he was calm. He told her he was sorry for yelling and helped her pick them up.

At breakfast, when his dad sat down and talked to him about his bad attitude the day before, Max felt his skin get prickly. But he took deep breaths until the feeling went away.

At the bus stop, Tim was already waiting for him, leaning against the telephone pole with his eyes half closed. He looked up when Max walked over. "Hi, Max."

"Hey, Tim." Max yawned.

They stood quietly. Neither knew what to say. Tim dug in the dirt with the toe of his shoe.

"So, how long have you been a werewolf?" Max asked.

"Um... about a year."

"Killed any zombies?"

"Well... a couple. They don't want me to fight much. Not until I can control myself. I only turned into a wolf ten times now. Only during the full moon." He shrugged. "I need more practice."

"Only ten times?"

"There's usually one full moon each month. You need to get a calendar and mark the days, so you know when you'll have to change."

"Can't we change other times?"

Tim made a face. "Why would you want to?"

"So we can practice."

"We're supposed to practice not getting mad. That's what Peter said will help."

The bus came then. They climbed in and sat in the

back as usual. Max was thinking, though. If he could turn into a wolf any time, he could practice controlling himself as a wolf. That had to help, right?

EIGHT

Secret Plan

Max tried his best to control his anger at school, all the way until recess. At recess, he saw the bully, Dean, in a corner of the field with his friends. They were all looking at the ground and laughing. Max walked over to them.

"What are you doing?" he asked.

"None of your business!" Dean said. He wrinkled up his nose and curled his lip. "Go away."

Something on the ground squealed in front of them.

"What are you doing?" Max asked again, louder this time. Dean turned around and ignored Max. He poked a long stick at something brown and furry by the fence. It squealed again and Dean's friends laughed.

It was a rabbit. Its fuzzy white belly was moving quickly. Its mouth was open. Its little arms were up in the air, trying to fight off the stick that was jabbing at it.

"Poke it in the eye!" One of Dean's friends laughed.

"Stop!" Max shoved past the kids. He stood between them and the rabbit. "Leave it alone!" He started to see red. His skin prickled. His chest felt tight.

"Why don't you go play with your baby toys?" one of the kids said.

"Go eat a poop sandwich!" Dean sneered.

Dean's friends all laughed.

Max saw Tim on the other side of the playground. Tim shook his head, telling Max not to do it.

Dean swung his stick, trying to hit Max in the face. Max grabbed the stick out of Dean's hand and threw it to the ground.

Then Max growled. Only it didn't sound like a boy's growl. He sounded like a monster. He felt his teeth growing into fangs. He opened his mouth wide and roared at the bullies.

Dean and his friends screamed and ran away.

Max closed his eyes and took two deep breaths. He cooled down. His skin stopped prickling. His chest didn't feel tight anymore. Then he turned around and looked at the rabbit.

The little rabbit was next to the fence. It sat very still, breathing fast.

Max didn't know what to do, but he thought the rabbit shouldn't be on the playground. Dean would find it and hurt it some more. So, Max picked up the rabbit, carried it to a hole in the fence, and let it out.

The rabbit sat looking at him for a second, then it hopped away through the trees.

After school, Max sat next to Tim on the bus ride home.

"Max, you aren't supposed to do things like that."

"Why not?"

"You're supposed to try not to be a wolf! You're supposed to stay calm!"

"But, did you see what they were doing?"

"Yeah, it was bad. But you can't just go wolf on them. You could hurt someone."

"I didn't hurt them." Max was angry. He kind of wanted to hurt the bullies. He knew that was bad, but it was true.

"If you don't practice, you'll still be dangerous when the full moon comes."

"All right." Max frowned. "Hey, do your mom and dad know you're a werewolf?"

Tim looked away and frowned. "No. We can't tell anyone about it."

"Why not?"

"If they believed us, they would send us to be studied for science. Or we'd be locked up in jail. Then who would fight the zombies?"

"That's true, I guess."

Max asked Tim questions all the way home. He wanted to learn all about being a werewolf. But he didn't tell Tim what he was really thinking. Max had a secret plan. That night, he would run away. He would go so far into the woods that he wouldn't be a danger to anyone. Then he would try to go wolf by himself.

NINE

Sneaking Out

THE REST of the day seemed to take forever. When he got home, Max had to finish a page of division problems for homework. Then he had to do his chores. He put away his laundry, took out the trash, and set the table for dinner. Max kept looking at the clock the whole time, wishing the hour hand would move faster. After dinner, he took a shower, and then, while everyone else was getting ready for bed, he sneaked his coat up to his room.

When it was time to go to sleep, Max stayed awake in his room with the light off. It wasn't easy. He was tired after all that happened that day and not getting much sleep the night before. But he was eager to go out and try his secret plan, too.

After what seemed like hours, he heard his mom and

dad turn off the downstairs lights, walk up the stairs and close their bedroom door.

Max waited to make sure they weren't going to come back out again. After he counted to a hundred and it was still quiet, he decided it was time.

Quietly, he climbed out of bed. He put on warm clothes, shoes, and his coat. He slid his window up and listened.

The house was still quiet. With his new super-sensitive ears, Max could hear the soft breathing of his sisters and parents in their bedrooms.

Max climbed out of his window and closed it most of the way, leaving it open a tiny bit so he could get back in. Then he jumped to the ground.

Being alone outside in the dark was scary. Not as scary as being a werewolf, but still scary. What if someone saw him and told his mom and dad? He crept through the shadows and tried to avoid passing in front of windows, but he still worried. Maybe someone would look in his room and see he wasn't there. What would he tell them if they caught him?

Max started to run. He went up the hill and past the park, through the trees and into the woods. He ran for a long time, but he never got tired. Finally, he was back at the grassy field.

It was a big open space. It felt even bigger without all

the other werewolves there. The moon sat low in the sky and was still almost round. Its silver light made Max feel weird. He wanted to run and bite and hit things.

Max closed his eyes, gritted his teeth, and concentrated. "C'mon. Change!"

Nothing happened.

He got down on his hands and knees and growled.

Still nothing.

He hit the ground with his fists. He howled at the moon with his human voice. He scratched his skin and rolled in the grass like a dog. It didn't work.

Max sat down and hugged his knees. Why didn't it work? What was he doing wrong?

He thought about when he went wolf the night before. He had been mad. At school, when he felt the change starting, he'd been mad then, too.

Maybe he needed to get mad?

He thought about the bullies. Dean had poked that poor rabbit. He was going to stab it in the eye with a stick. Dean had laughed at the helpless little thing when it squealed.

Max started to feel it. He looked up at the moon and let himself be mad. He let the anger take him.

The sky went red. His skin burned. The monster exploded in his chest. Max the werewolf stood in the moonlight.

TEN

Lone Wolf

BEING a wolf was different this time. Max didn't feel wild or scared. He felt good.

Max walked around the field, trying out his wolf body. The grass crunched under his paws. The air felt icy on his nose, but the cold didn't bother him. He could even see in the dark under the trees. It all looked red, but it was clear as day. He sniffed at all the interesting scents in the air and snorted when he smelled a dead skunk nearby and the trash cans left out to be collected in the morning.

Some of the smells made his mouth water. But even though he was hungry, Max didn't run to eat them like last time. He knew they might be people.

Max shook his fur and walked further into the woods where people usually didn't go. He followed one of the enticing smells on the wind. After a little while, he found a flock of sleeping turkeys.

Max licked his chops. He crouched down and crept closer and closer to a big, fat one near the trees. He made almost no sound as he approached within inches of the sleeping bird. Then, in a flash, he snapped it up in his jaws.

The turkey squawked and flapped its wings. The others startled and flew away, scattering feathers all over. Max crunched down on the bird's neck and it went still.

Eating the turkey made Max feel a little better. Being a wolf made him hungry, and the bird tasted really good, even if it did have a lot of feathers that he had to pick out of his teeth.

Max explored the woods for a while longer, making sure to stay hidden behind trees and bushes. He found one old graveyard with glowing green mist over the ground. It smelled like rotten meat, but he didn't understand what it was.

In the end, he changed back to a boy and went to bed to get some much-needed sleep. He felt pleased with his first test as a werewolf. He didn't hurt any people and he had learned a lot.

The next day at recess, he took Tim aside and told him what he'd done.

"Are you crazy?" Tim asked. "You went wolf by yourself? What if you killed someone?"

"I didn't. It was easy."

Tim narrowed his eyes like he didn't believe it.

"I did eat a turkey, but that's all. I just looked around."

"You really didn't hurt anyone?"

"No, I was far away from all the houses. And I made sure it was a turkey and not a person before I ate it."

Tim's eyes went wide. "How did you do it?"

"What?"

"How did you not try to eat people?"

Max shrugged. "Maybe it's because it wasn't a full moon?"

Tim nodded. "I guess that might help. I never tried it before."

Max had a great idea. "You can try it tonight!" He was so excited, it didn't matter that he was already tired from staying up so late. "Huh?"

"Let's sneak out and go wolf together. I found some cool stuff to show you. It'll be so fun!"

Tim looked worried but excited too. He bit his lip and looked around. "I don't know..."

"Did you ever catch your own food before?"

Tim shrugged. "Not really."

Max smiled. "I'll show you how to catch a turkey."

Tim hesitated a little longer, biting his lip. Then he sighed. "Okay. I'll do it. We can meet at the park after midnight."

"Then we'll walk to the field to go wolf. That way there won't be any people close," Max said.

Tim nodded. "Good idea."

"Great!"

"Don't tell Peter, though!" Tim still looked nervous. "He'll be so mad if he finds out."

ELEVEN

Daring Duo

Max's mom made a pot roast for dinner that night. He ate all his meat and then kept going back for more.

His mom laughed. "You're as hungry as a wolf tonight, aren't you?"

Max took another big bite and grinned at her.

"Well, leave some for everyone else," she said.

Max finished all the food on his plate and even polished off what his sisters didn't eat.

After dinner he put on his warmest pajamas and sneaked his coat up to his room again while his mom and dad got his sisters ready for bed.

Max struggle to stayed awake while he waited for the house to get quiet. Then, just like last time, he opened his window and crawled out.

Tim was waiting for him at the park, just as they had planned. He sat on the bottom of the slide with his hands in his pockets.

"Hi, Max." He looked scared.

"Hi, Tim. You ready?"

"Yeah." Tim got up and they walked into the woods together.

"Hey, Tim, how did you get to be a werewolf?" Max asked.

Tim looked surprised. "I got bit, just like you."

"Yeah, but who bit you? How did it happen?"

Tim thought about it for a minute. "I was out with some kids at night. We were riding bikes. It was getting dark, and they dared me to ride through the graveyard alone."

Tim broke a small branch off a tree and hacked the bushes with it.

"Who were they?" Max asked.

"They're in fifth grade now. It doesn't matter. They tricked me. They let me go in but left me there."

Tim hacked at a small bush so hard it snapped in half. He threw his stick into the trees.

"I saw that they were gone, but before I could get out of there, something weird happened. There was glowing green mist everywhere. It smelled... gross. Really bad. Then zombies started digging out of the ground."

"Really? You saw zombies?" Max grinned.

"Yeah," Tim laughed at how excited Max was about zombies. "They started to come for me. Then the werewolves showed up. The wolves fought the zombies, but there were a lot of them."

Tim paused and frowned at the memory. "A couple zombies grabbed me. It was super gross and super scary at the same time. A wolf came to fight them off, but she bit me by accident, too."

They had reached the field in the woods. Max looked up at the moon and took a deep breath. "You know, I think it's kind of cool that we're werewolves."

"Really? It isn't easy. Remember how I almost killed you?"

"Oh, that's no big deal." Max laughed.

After a while, Tim laughed, too. "Okay, let's go wolf. You can show me how easy it is to be in control." He closed his eyes tight shut. He looked angry for a second. Then he changed. His body grew big. His clothes turned into thick fur. His hands turned into big paws. He grew a tail. His face grew longer, and his teeth grew into sharp fangs.

There was a wolf in the field with Max now. It shook its head and growled. "Change, Max, hurry! I might attack you!"

Max thought hard. What did he do to change? Oh, that's right, he had to feel mad.

Tim dug into the ground with his sharp claws. He showed his white teeth. "Change, Max!"

He had to get mad. What could he get mad at? He couldn't think with Tim drooling and growling next to him.

Tim took a step toward Max. He snapped his teeth. Drool dripped from his lips. "Change now!"

"Stop! I'm trying! I can't think with you growling at me like that!"

That did it.

Max felt anger burn in his chest. His vision went red. His face got hot. His skin prickled. The wolf burst out from inside him.

TWELVE

The Chase

It wasn't easy this time. Max felt anger twist in his brain like a worm. The world suddenly sounded too loud. He was hungry and scared and felt crazy. He couldn't think the way he had the night before.

"Max? You okay?"

Max snarled at Tim. He snapped his teeth and started running.

"No! Max, no!" Tim chased him through the trees.

Max followed the tasty smells on the wind, but Tim kept getting in the way, cutting him off and making him change directions. He tried to run faster, but Tim kept up with him. Tim knew the woods better than Max did. Max couldn't lose him. And Max couldn't think straight anyway. For a long time, Tim just chased Max while Max tried to get away.

Finally, Max started to feel a little tired. He also felt a little less mad and scared. He was still hungry, but he could think better now. He stopped running and Tim stopped with him.

They were on the edge of some woods, near an old, empty church building with broken windows.

"Can you change back?" Tim asked.

"Out here? How would we get home?" Max said. He still wasn't very good at speaking with his wolf mouth, but Tim understood him anyway.

"I don't know, but it's better than chasing you all night to keep you from killing."

"I'm fine now."

"No, you're not!"

No, he wasn't. But Max didn't want to say it. He gnashed his teeth and dug his claws into the ground in frustration.

"I'm going to call for help," Tim said.

"How?"

Tim put his head back and howled loud and long. *AwoooOOOOoooo.*

His howl echoed through the trees and out along the hills.

"Are you telling on me?" Max growled.

"I have to! I can barely control myself. I can't keep you safe all night."

"I don't need a babysitter!"

"Yes, you do!"

They snarled at each other. The fur stood up on their backs. They showed their fangs.

Then, out on the lawn by the old church, a glowing green mist formed. It floated over the ground between the crumbling old gravestones. It crept low, spreading out until the werewolves smelled it.

Tim stopped growling and looked up, sniffing the mist. "No way!"

"What?" Max snapped.

"That mist—that green mist—it makes the zombies!"

Max stopped growling and looked at the mist. "I saw some of that last night."

"You did?"

"I didn't see any zombies, though."

"Come on." Tim walked out into the field. Max followed.

The glowing green mist really did smell bad. It smelled worse than rotten meat, sour milk, and even Mia's squishy, still-warm dirty diapers. The hair stood up on their backs as they walked over the graves.

Tim shook his fur out. "This is really creepy."

"Said the werewolf! Ha!"

"Can you feel it?" Tim patted the ground with his front paws.

Max did feel it. Something was moving deep under the dirt. Max thought about what was buried there and gulped. He didn't want to stick around and see what it was.

All of a sudden, a hand dug out of the grave next to them. It grabbed at the dirt and started to pull its body out.

Max and Tim backed away. But more arms started digging out all around them.

"Zombies!" Tim howled.

"Should we fight them?"

"Alone?!"

Dead bodies crumbled out of the dirt. Their flesh varied from muddy yellow to sickly green and grey. Their bones showed through their skin. Their clothes were rotten. Pieces of their bodies dropped off onto the ground. They smelled even worse than the mist that still filled the air. The zombies started shuffling toward the two werewolves.

THIRTEEN

Banshees

MAX JUMPED onto the nearest zombie and tore it to pieces. It tasted worse than he ever thought it would. He gagged and wanted to puke. But more zombies were coming.

Tim jumped a little away from Max to give him space. A group of zombies grabbed him, and he ripped them to pieces.

The werewolves bit and kicked and tore at the crowds of dead bodies. Max tried to use his claws so he could keep the rotting flesh out of his mouth. But sometimes he had to bite anyway, and it was awful. Especially when he ended up with a mouth full of squishy, rotten zombie brains.

Max and Tim fought like wild beasts, not thinking, just destroying. Max felt rage growing inside him. A group of zombies surrounded him and attacked from all sides. Max tried to throw them off. He flung his body in a circle, but the zombies clung to him like leeches. A few of them bit into his flesh with their rotten teeth. Max yelped in pain. A few yards away, he saw Tim covered in zombies, too. He was rolling on the ground to try to get them off.

Then something changed. Three women in long dresses floated over the graveyard. They had wild black hair and skin white like paper. Their eyes were black behind dark bruises. Their lips were as red as blood. Max saw them and realized they must be the banshees Peter had told him about. But he couldn't do anything about them when he was covered with zombies.

The two werewolves fought the swarms of zombies clinging to them in a mindless frenzy. For every zombie they destroyed, another latched on. Their bites were small and healed fast. But with so many attacking at once, it was starting to add up and really hurt.

They didn't pay attention to the floating women getting closer. But then the banshees opened their mouths, showing their long, pointed teeth, and screamed.

Max and Tim, along with the zombies clinging to them, flew through the air and landed on the ground. The zombies fell to pieces with the force of the blow.

Max felt the scream tear right through his body. Max and Tim howled in pain.

Max couldn't get up. It felt like all the bones in his body were broken. The banshees moved closer. Their hair flew around their faces like they were floating underwater. Max could see the pointed teeth inside their red mouths. He was sure they were about to die. He tried to get up in spite of the pain and terror, but he couldn't.

Suddenly, a huge werewolf jumped between Max and the banshees. The large wolf snarled. The fur stood up on his back as he took a slow step forward. More wolves came. Three more. Five more. Soon, the entire graveyard seemed filled with werewolves.

Max watched the wolves attack. They jumped on the zombies, biting off heads, scratching them to pieces, dashing them against trees and rocks. The older wolves fought the zombies easily, destroying the whole mob of them in a few seconds.

Then some attacked the banshees, but the banshees moved too fast. The floating ghost-like monsters screamed again. Four of the werewolves yelped and fell to the ground. The two who were left jumped at them. But the banshees just dodged the attack and flew away into the night.

After a few minutes of lying still, Max started to feel

a little better. He pushed himself up onto his paws. Next to him, Tim also stood.

Two werewolves towered over them, watching. He recognized Peter, but the other was one of the wolves Max didn't know yet. The four hurt by the banshees still lay on the ground. Max felt sorry for them. But he was so amped up from fighting that he wished there were still more zombies to kill.

Peter growled quietly. In the dark, standing over them, he looked very big and very black. His eyes glowed red as he stared down at Max and Tim.

"What were you doing out here?"

Tim whined.

But Max growled back. He thought he'd fought the zombies pretty well for his first time, at least until the banshees showed up. Why was Peter angry?

The other wolves were standing up now. They gathered close to listen.

"We were practicing," Max said.

"Practicing? You two? Alone! Tim, you know better!"

Tim lay on the ground. He put his front paws over his nose in shame. "Max said he could control it. He said it was easy."

"Is that so?"

Max growled again. The crazy anger he felt as a

werewolf still burned in his mind. Everything made him mad.

"It was easy yesterday. I went wolf by myself and I didn't hurt anyone!"

The other wolves looked at each other, surprised.

Peter growled. "That can't be! That's impossible!"

"It's true. It felt different last night! I didn't even try to hurt anyone."

Peter closed his eyes and took deep breaths. "You two were very foolish tonight. We're taking you home now."

FOURTEEN

Walk of Shame

MAX AND TIM walked next to each other. They were surrounded by the other wolves. Peter stayed in front of the pack, leading them.

When they were back in the woods near Max's house, one of the other wolves came close.

"Hey, kid, is it true?" she asked.

"Huh?"

"Did you really change last night? Alone?"

"Yeah. I did."

"He's lying, Becca," another one said. She also sounded like a girl. "He just wants to impress us."

"I'm not lying!" Max snapped.

"If you did," she said. "Then you would have gone wild. You would have killed everyone you met. That's what you would do right now if we left you alone."

Max growled at her, but he knew she was right. He hadn't been able to control himself this time. If Tim hadn't been with him, he would have eaten all those people. He really was a monster.

"Why is it different now?" he asked. "I didn't have trouble last night. Why am I crazy this time?"

The two wolves snorted and shook their heads. They didn't believe him.

"I wish it was true," another wolf behind them said.

"Forget it, Lucas," the second girl wolf said. "You know it never works." She turned to Max. "There is no easy way to control your anger. You just have to practice when you're a person."

Lucas sighed. "I didn't mean that, Katie. I was just saying—"

"Well don't. Don't put ideas into their heads. There's been too much trouble already."

Max growled again. "I'm not lying. I ran around. I ate a turkey. I saw some green mist. Then I came home. That's it!"

"Ooh!" Lucas said. "Turkeys are good. But deer are my favorite." He licked his lips. "Don't worry about my sister, Kate. She's always like this."

Kate growled at him.

"That's enough!" Peter snarled. "We're close to your

houses now. Max and Tim, change back and go home."
He glared at Max.

Max cringed and Peter's gaze softened a little. "Get
some sleep. But meet us here again tomorrow night. We
need to talk about what happened."

Max and Tim nodded and changed back. Max felt
more in control of himself once he was human again. He
still remembered the crazy anger and hunger driving
him to eat anyone he could smell and shuddered. Could
he really be such a monster?

It was cold without their thick wolf fur. Max pulled
his coat around himself and they started walking home.

Tim was quiet.

"I wasn't lying, Tim. You believe me, right?"

"It didn't work. You were wrong."

"I know. I don't get it. Maybe I did something
different last time."

Tim didn't say anything.

"I'll find out what went wrong. I'll keep trying
and—"

"Stop, Max." Tim spoke quietly. He was trying not
to get mad. "Don't be stupid, okay? You were wrong. Just
listen to Peter. You'll end up killing people. Don't you
know that? What if it's your mom, or your dad, or your
sisters? Think about someone else for a change."

A wolfy growl rumbled in Max's chest at Tim's tone.

But then he thought of his family. What if he'd been closer to home when he changed? He didn't want to think he would hurt them, but he knew how he'd lost control as a wolf.

Tim sighed. "I'm sorry. I shouldn't have said that."

Max breathed hard as the last of his anger left him. "You're right. I don't want to hurt my family. I don't want to hurt anyone. Well, not usually."

Tim laughed. "There's plenty of zombies to kill."

Max made a grossed-out face. "Ew! Don't make me puke."

Max and Tim split up and walked to their homes. Max climbed into his room, took off his coat and shoes, and crawled into bed.

He knew Tim was right. He should listen to Peter. But he knew he was right too. He wasn't lying. There had to be a way to transform and not go crazy, and he would figure it out.

FIFTEEN

Go Wolf

When Max got to the field the next night, everyone was still human. It was strange to see them all as people rather than wolves.

Max knew who Tim and Peter were. But it took him a while to figure out who Lucas, Kate, and Becca were. There were eight werewolves total, including Max and Tim.

"We need to talk about our plan," Peter said. "All three banshees showed up and fought us last night. I don't know why, but it can't be good."

"Maybe they wanted an easy win," Kate said. She looked at Max and Tim. "They left when the rest of us got there."

"Maybe, but they might be getting stronger, too. For

the rest of this month, I want us to go out together. All of us. Every night."

"What?"

"No!"

"Come on!"

"Yes," Peter said. "We will go back to shifts after the next full moon if they have backed off. I don't want to put any of us at risk."

"Even tonight?" Tim asked.

"Yes, we need to patrol tonight, too. So, let's go. Oldest to youngest."

Max thought, at first, that oldest to youngest meant the old guy would change first. But it was Peter who went wolf before any of the others. He went to an open space, closed his eyes, growled, and suddenly he was a huge black wolf with red eyes.

Then Kate changed after him. Max realized that they were changing in the order they'd been bitten. That meant that he would go last of all.

He remembered that Peter said he'd been a werewolf for over a hundred years. Did that mean that they never got older? Would he never grow up? He'd have to ask about that sometime.

Max watched as Lucas changed, followed by the old man, and then the girl he didn't know. Finally, when

Max was surrounded by seven huge wolves, it was his turn.

He walked to the center of the field and looked up at the moon. He tried to feel the heat in his face. He tried to make his skin prickle. He closed his eyes and tried to think of something that would make him really mad.

What was it last time? He'd been mad at Tim for growling at him. And the time before that? He was mad at Dean for hurting the rabbit. Was there some difference in being mad at a bully and being mad at a friend? Or was it because he was mad for someone else the first time? He thought about what Tim said the other night. He shouldn't just think about himself.

"Come on, dude! Go wolf already!" Lucas growled. He swished his tail and jumped at Max.

Max tried to duck out of the way, but Lucas hit him with his nose. Max fell into the cold damp leaves.

"Back off!" Tim snarled at Lucas.

"No way! The little dude needs to learn!" He turned and barked a laugh at Max. "Are you a super-wolf or not? Come on and show us!"

He shoved Max with his nose again. A couple of the other wolves laughed.

"Come on. You can control it, can't you? Do it! Do it now!"

He pushed Max down again and again. Finally, Max had enough. Lucas came at Max one more time. Max roared and burst into a wolf.

SIXTEEN

Zombie Hunt

Max was wild with rage. He bit Lucas on the throat and shook him to the ground.

Lucas yelped in pain, rolled over, and kicked Max off with his back legs.

Max flew into a big tree. He hit it so hard the trunk cracked, and a few branches snapped off. Then he fell to the ground.

"Nice shot, kid." Lucas coughed and laughed a little. The fur on his neck was wet with blood. "You surprised me."

"That was really stupid," Becca snorted.

"What?" Lucas asked. "He needed help. Now we're all ready to go." Max snarled and barked at them. He was still crazy mad.

"We'll wait a few minutes for you to heal and for

Max to calm down," Peter said to Lucas, then he turned to talk to all of them.

"We're going to be running through the usual spots tonight. But this is Max's first time and Tim is still new. They'll need a guard. Frank, you stay behind them."

The old silver wolf nodded.

"Rachel and Becca, you stay on their flanks."

Two other wolves nodded.

"Lucas and Kate, you run in front with me."

Lucas and Kate nodded, too.

"All right. Does everyone know their place? How are you now, Lucas?"

"Fit to fight, captain!" Lucas grinned, showing off his fangs.

"And you, Max?"

Max crawled out from under the tree. He growled quietly at Lucas, still mad but trying to look calm.

"All right. You two stay in your place. If you try to run away, we'll take you down and you'll have to go home. Understand?"

Max and Tim nodded.

"Let's go."

Peter, Lucas, and Kate turned and started running through the trees. Max and Tim raced after them. Their guard wolves kept with them on all sides.

The werewolves ran far into the woods, much farther than Max had gone last time.

He smelled tasty scents in the wind. It made him hungry. He wanted to follow the smells and eat whatever they were. But the other werewolves wouldn't let him leave.

They came to a small graveyard. There was no green mist, so they ran past it. Then they came to another and another. After a while, Max started to wonder if there wasn't going to be any zombie fighting tonight.

Finally, they came to a large cemetery. There were hundreds of graves. Over all of them, the glowing green mist drifted low and thick.

"This is it, spread out," Peter called.

All the wolves went in different directions.

Max followed Tim. "What's going on?" he asked.

"We need to stay apart. We might attack each other by mistake if we're too close."

"I don't think—"

"Don't argue. Just go where you won't hurt anyone."

Max growled, but he ran off to an empty part of the cemetery.

He listened and looked around for the banshees. A cold wind blew over the gravestones. It made the stinky green mist swirl around his paws. Something moved under the ground. Max snarled and crouched, looking around, waiting. The hair on his back stood on end. His white fangs flashed in the dark.

The earth crumbled at his feet. He heard the sounds of zombies digging in every direction. He could smell their rotten flesh even from under the surface. A hand and a skull pushed out of the ground in front of him. Mud was packed in the holes where its eyes used to be.

Max snarled. He heard the other werewolves growling, clawing, and biting around him.

Max jumped on the zombie and crushed its skull between his teeth.

SEVENTEEN

Epic Carnage

MAX FOUGHT LIKE MAD. The whole world looked red. Nasty zombie brains splattered everywhere. His nose was full of it. His fur dripped with green and yellow slime. He didn't stop to think, he just snapped, and tore, and crunched, and ripped anything that moved near him.

The other werewolves did the same. Max could see and hear them fighting all around him.

It made sense now how Tim had gotten bit. Max wouldn't be able to keep from attacking anything that was near a zombie, not now that he was fighting. He couldn't think about what he was doing at all. He could only kill.

Then the banshees came. This time, all the wolves were there and fighting. Peter charged and three other wolves followed him. One of the banshees screamed and a wolf fell to the ground. The other two werewolves jumped at her. She dodged the attack. Then all three banshees turned and flew away into the trees.

The glowing mist faded. The zombie attack stopped. The bodies around them crumbled into dust and sludge.

The zombies were gone, but Max was so crazy he couldn't stop fighting. He ran in circles. He tore up the slimy ground with his claws. He kicked over tombstones and ripped branches from the trees with his teeth.

The werewolves slowly calmed down, one by one.

When Max could think again, he went to join Peter and the others. They all met behind a big stone building far from the road. Every one of them was dripping with stink and slime.

"It happens every time we fight them," Peter said. He spat out a mouthful of green sludge. "The banshees are too fast. They always fly away."

"What if we set a trap for them?" Max asked.

Tim shook some slime out of his fur and looked at him. "What kind of trap?"

"We could split up. Some of us can chase them, and some can be waiting to get them when they fly away."

Peter shook his head. "It won't work. We can't do things together like that."

"Think about it," Becca said, rubbing zombie ooze off her nose with a paw. "How did it feel tonight when you were fighting?"

Max thought about it. "I was really mad. I couldn't stop, even when I wanted to."

"It's like that for all of us," she told him. "We can't set a trap. We can't even think straight during a fight."

Peter nodded. "We could try to make a plan, but no one would remember it once the zombies came."

"So, it would work if we were in control?"

"It doesn't matter," Peter growled. "We can't do it. I

know because I've been a werewolf longer than your parents have been alive."

"But—"

"That's enough!" Peter snapped. "You didn't find some magical way to control yourself, because there is no way. If there was a way to do it, I would have found it out long ago."

Max snarled and growled. He bared his teeth at Peter. His slimy fur stood on end.

Peter just ignored him. "We'll meet in the field again tomorrow night. Maybe the banshees will turn up again and we'll get another shot at them. For now, let's go wash off this stink."

They all walked down to the waterfront. The rocks along the shore were white and crunchy with frost. The wolves waded in and rinsed off the zombie slime as well as they could before heading home.

EIGHTEEN

Facing bullies

EVEN AFTER THE werewolves washed in the water, some of the zombie stink stuck to them. Max's mom held her nose when he opened his bedroom door in the morning.

"Ew! Max! What is that smell?" She waved her hand in front of her nose to blow it away. "Were you playing in a trash can or something? Go take a shower. Use lots of soap, too."

At school, Max spent a lot of time thinking. He didn't understand why he went so crazy when he was fighting the zombies. Was it only a dream that he'd been in control that one night when he was alone?

Miss Diaz called on him to answer a question in class. Max got the answer wrong because he wasn't paying attention. Dean and his friends laughed at him and Max glared at them.

At recess, Max ran to the swings with Tim so they could get there before anyone else. They swung together for a while, seeing who could go the highest. When the teachers got scared and told them not to go so high, they slowed down.

"Tim, do you think we'll ever beat the banshees?" Max asked.

"Yeah, of course."

"But... How long has Peter been trying to kill them?"

"I don't know. A long time. But there are more of us now. Don't worry. We'll get them."

"How, if we can't fight close to each other? Peter says they always get away."

"Yeah, but—"

"What if they find a way to hide? What if we can't find them one night? What if they hurt our families?"

Tim frowned. He dragged his feet to stop his swing.

"I wasn't lying before," Max said. "It was different that time. I could control myself. If we could work as a team, we would win easy! We could get them!"

"But you don't know how you did it. And if you go wolf alone, you might kill your family yourself."

Max frowned, but not at what Tim had said. He was looking past Tim now, to the corner of the playground by the big tree. Dean was there with some of his friends. They were laughing at a girl who was sitting by herself.

Max got up and ran over to them. Tim jumped up and followed him.

"Look. These are all my friends," Dean said to the girl. "So where are your friends? You don't have any, do you?"

The girl's face was red. "They... don't go to this school," she mumbled.

"Yeah, right!" Dean laughed. He picked up a clump of dirt and threw it at her. It smacked her face. Some of the dirt stuck behind her glasses. The girl started to cry and rubbed the dirt off of her face.

Dean's friends laughed. One of the girls with him also picked up a handful of dirt and threw it at the crying girl.

"Hey, stop it!" Tim shouted.

Max and Tim stood between the bullies and the girl.

"Hey look," Dean laughed. "It's the freak and his loser friend! What are you going to do, yell at us again?"

The other bullies laughed, too.

"Leave her alone," Tim said.

Max heard a deep rumble in Tim's voice. He felt his own face getting hot. His guts were getting tight.

Dean tried to shove past them. Max and Tim each grabbed an arm and pushed him back. Dean was bigger than they were, but they had no trouble pushing him over. He was so light he felt like he was made of balloons. Dean tripped backward and crashed into the other bullies. They all tumbled down together in a pile on the ground.

NINETEEN

A Big Risk

Max was glad when Dean got in trouble for bullying. Max and Tim got in trouble for fighting at school, too, but it was worth it. As they sat outside the office, he knew Tim was upset about it, but it didn't bother Max. He didn't even care when the school called his mom.

Fighting Dean had given Max an idea. He knew if he told the other werewolves, they wouldn't let him try it. So he had to keep it a secret. He wouldn't even tell Tim, at least not until he knew it worked.

Back at home, Mia didn't want to sit in her chair for dinner. She kept crying and throwing her food on the floor.

Maddie tried to make her laugh. She crawled under the table and jumped out, shouting, "Peekaboo! Peekaboo!" But Mia just cried.

"Am I funny Mia? Look at me!" Maddie made goofy faces.

"No! Go way!" Mia yelled.

"It's okay, sweetie. Just leave her be," his mom said. She nudged Maddie back to her seat.

"Mia, let's have a better attitude, young lady," his dad said.

Mia crossed her arms and turned away.

"I don't know what's with her," his mom said. "It must be a full moon tonight."

"It's not a full moon," Max said.

"Oh, really?" his dad asked.

"Nope, the next one isn't until April eighth."

"Huh, no kidding! How do you know that?"

"I... um... I just looked it up." On his calendar in his room, Max had circled all the days the moon would be full. Peter had told them that on normal nights, they *could* go wolf. But on nights with a full moon, it happened whether they wanted it or not. So, Max had to go with the other wolves or stay out of the moonlight on those nights.

"Do you want any more noodles?" his mom asked.

"No, thanks. Can I go play in my room now?"

"You need to finish your chores first. Don't forget," his dad said. Max frowned and stabbed another meatball with his fork. "All right."

It took him a long time to finish all his chores. He wiped the table after dinner. He read a story to his sisters. He put away his laundry. He did his homework. He brushed his teeth. By the time he had finished everything, it was time to go to bed.

Max said goodnight to his sisters and to his mom and dad. Then he closed his door and started his plan.

He stuffed pillows under his blankets. If his mom or dad came to check on him, it would look like he was still in bed. He pulled on his boots. He slid his arms into his coat and zipped it up. Then, very carefully, he pulled his window open and climbed out.

It was raining outside. Drops of water hit his cheeks and hands like ice.

Max slid the window down until it was almost closed. Then he dropped to the ground.

The lights were still on in his house. He looked through the window and saw his dad washing dishes. The clock on the stove said it was a little after eight. He still had plenty of time.

Max ran through the dark up the street. Cold rain pelted his face. He ran past the playground and into the trees.

He knew he was taking a big risk. Still, if he was right, this would change everything.

No one else was there yet when Max got to the field. The grass was soggy. Mud squished under his boots.

Max looked up at the moon. He remembered how Dean had hurt the rabbit, and how he threw dirt at the girl on the playground. The memory made him mad, but not mad enough. His skin prickled.

The moon was smaller tonight. It was only about half full, so it was harder to feel angry now.

Then he remembered the banshees. He remembered how badly it hurt when they screamed at him. He thought about his parents and his sisters. They couldn't heal like he could now. What if the banshees killed his family?

He imagined the banshees flying over his house. He imagined them creeping through the window where his sisters slept. He imagined them screaming at Maddie and Mia.

Max roared at the moon. His guts got tight. His face burned. He burst into a werewolf.

TWENTY

Good News

MAX KNEW RIGHT AWAY that he'd done it. He still felt a little angry, but he was in control. He didn't feel like running away to eat people.

He barked a wolfy laugh through his teeth. "Ha ha! I knew it!"

He had to stop himself from howling with joy. Peter and the others might hear him.

"So, you really did do it."

Max whipped his head around and saw Lucas and Kate walking toward him over the soggy grass.

Lucas laughed. "Katie and I thought you might come out here and try something."

Kate grinned. "We're here to stop you from murdering the villagers if it didn't work."

"Are you going to tell Peter?" Max asked.

"Isn't that the point? Don't you want to show him it's possible?" Kate asked.

"I just want you all to know how to do it. Then we can fight together."

Lucas and Kate looked at each other then back at Max.

"All right, then," Lucas said.

"How did you do it?" Kate asked.

Max wagged his tail. "It's easy. You just have to be mad for someone else."

"Huh?"

Max tilted his head, trying to think of how to explain it. "I was mad at a bully for hurting a rabbit the first time it worked. Tonight, I was mad thinking that the banshees would hurt my family. Get mad, but not for yourself."

"Hmm." Lucas scratched his head. "I can't believe I never tried that before."

"I'll try it now," Kate said. She ran to the middle of the field and closed her eyes, but nothing happened.

Lucas laughed at her.

"It's harder than it sounds!" she said.

Lucas went out next to her and tried to do it. He also had trouble. Max walked around the field for a while, waiting for them.

It took a few minutes. Lucas and Kate both had trouble thinking of something that made them angry enough. But then Kate suddenly went wolf, and Lucas did it a few seconds after her. Three werewolves stood in the field, grinning with their sharp teeth.

After Max's trick worked for them, they decided to find the others. Kate and Lucas said they should show Becca, Frank, and Rachel first, since they were older and had been werewolves longer than Max and Tim had. It took a couple of hours to find them and convince them to try the new trick. When it worked for them, too, they all agreed that Max should be the one to find Tim and tell him to meet them all in the woods.

Max crept up to Tim's house in the dark. The pouring rain dripped from his fur, making him an even darker shade of black than usual. Through the downstairs window, he could see Tim's mom and dad watching TV in the living room. The rest of the lights in the house were off, though. So Max circled around to the back and climbed up the siding and onto the roof. He peered down into Tim's window and saw that his friend was awake and reading a book with a flashlight.

Max chuckled, imagining how Tim was going to freak out about this.

He lowered his paw over the ledge and tapped on Tim's window with one long claw.

He heard Tim move inside, but his friend didn't

come to the window, so Max lowered his paw and tapped again.

This time, Tim jumped out of bed and opened his window, poking his face out and looking at Max. His eyes were wide with fear.

"Come out, Tim. We have something to show you!" Max could barely contain his laughter.

Tim didn't answer. His mouth opened wide and his face went pale.

"Come on! Meet us in the woods. Hurry!" Max jumped off the roof, twisted in the air and landed with a low splat on the wet grass. He shook the rain from his fur and looked back up at Tim, who was still staring at him in shock.

Max grinned, then turned and ran up the street.

TWENTY-ONE

Part of the Pack

Max was waiting in the clearing with most of the other wolves when Tim joined them. The other werewolves sat and watched him as he approached. But none of them looked angry or about to bite.

Max walked forward to meet him, wagging his tail. His paws squished in the muddy grass. "Hi, Tim. Guess what!"

"What are you doing, Max?" Tim yelled. "Why did you come to my house? You could have killed my family? Are you stupid or what?"

"Wait!" Max barked. "Listen—"

"Don't ever come to my house as a wolf again!" Tim's voice was low, but rumbled with a deep wolf growl.

Then Max had an idea. He lowered his furry head to Tim's level and grinned with his sharp fangs.

"I probably will. It's no big deal."

"What?!" Tim shouted. He clenched his fists as his sides so hard his knuckles went white.

"I'll come and get you as a wolf sometimes. I'm sure I won't hurt your parents. They'll never even know I was there!"

Tim growled. He squeezed his eyes shut. Then he burst into his wolf form and jumped at Max with his fangs bared.

They bit and snapped at each other for a few seconds. Then Max kicked Tim off and barked at him. "Stop. Just listen to me!"

Tim crouched low, showing his teeth. His ears were flat on his head. The fur on his back stood on end. He snarled and growled from deep in his chest.

"How do you feel?" Max asked.

"Stay away from my family!" Tim snarled.

"Okay," Max said. "But other than that, how do you feel? Do you want to eat anyone?"

Tim paused for a second, blinking. Then he relaxed and stood up straight. "No, I don't." He turned to the other wolves.

They all sat, calm and smiling, while they watched him.

"Wow... I... I'm in control?"

"Yeah!" Max laughed. "I figured it out! You just have to be mad for someone else!"

Tim's ears went up and he wagged his tail. "Seriously? I was totally ready to rip your throat out! But this is so cool!"

"I know! Right?" Lucas barked. He laughed and pounced on Tim. They rolled and kicked, playing like dogs. Max and Kate jumped in, too. After a while, Becca, Rachel, and Frank joined them. The whole pack was rolling in the mud, tackling and kicking, growling and laughing. For the first time since becoming a werewolf, Max felt like he was really a part of the pack. Like he belonged with them.

"What's going on here?"

Everyone stopped at the sound of Peter's voice. They stood up and faced him, their fur caked with mud and dead grass.

Peter walked into the field still on two feet, not in his wolf form yet. He narrowed his eyes at the group of muddy werewolves.

Max gulped and his ears flattened against his head. He looked around at the others and then back at Peter. "Um, I found out how to do it. We all did. We're in control now."

Peter looked up at all the muddy werewolves around him. He still looked angry. "Is that so?"

TWENTY-TWO

Plan of Attack

The rest of the pack waited while Max told Peter what was going on.

Peter listened quietly and looked at all of them while Max explained. Then when Max had finished, he said, "All right. I'll try it."

He seemed to have no trouble at all. Peter just walked to the open space in the middle of the field, and two seconds later he morphed into a big, black hairy werewolf.

Peter took two slow breaths and blinked. Then his eyes turned to Max. "It's true."

Max nodded.

"All this time... I didn't know." Peter's voice sounded strained. He looked to the ground, took a deep breath, and looked back at Max.

The rest of the pack walked to him and sat in a circle around their leader.

"Max... I'm sorry I didn't listen to you. You are a new wolf and a child. I was afraid that you would hurt yourself or others. And I never dreamed that this was really possible."

"You're not mad?"

Peter laughed once and then sighed. "Of course, I'm mad. You went off by yourself and changed. You didn't know if it would work or not. You could have killed someone and none of the other wolves would have been here to stop you."

Max curled his tail under himself and lowered his nose in shame.

"But it's that anger that made me change into a wolf this time. Now I'm in control, and I can see that I was wrong, too. So, we'll talk about your foolish actions later. Right now, we have a war to fight."

"All right!" Lucas jumped up and landed in a crouch on all four paws. "Let's rip up some zombies!"

"It will be good to finally see the end of them," the old wolf, Frank, said. His silver fur was almost all brown and black with mud.

"We might have a chance at winning now," Becca said.

"I have an idea," Peter said. "I've been watching them all these years and I think I know how we can beat them. Listen..."

Peter explained his plan of attack. Each wolf had a role to play. The plan required teamwork, so Max listened carefully, trying his best to memorize where each member of the pack would be at every phase of the plan. If they wanted to pull it off, they would have to work together.

When Peter finished explaining, they set out to look for their enemy.

It was more fun traveling as a pack without that crazy rage filling up his brain. Max could feel the breeze blowing through his fur. He could enjoy the smells of the trees and plants and the animals cowering in their burrows as they passed. He could hear interesting sounds on the wind, from the cars driving up the road to the bats screeching as they caught bugs over a pond.

The pack ran closer to the towns than they had the last time. Max could smell the pizza cooking in a corner restaurant, smog from cars driving past, and lots of people. The people still smelled tasty, but he didn't want to eat them anymore. None of the other werewolves seemed to either.

They ran for almost an hour and came across six

different graveyards. None of them had the green mist, so they ran past and on to others. Max wondered if Peter had memorized the location of every single graveyard in the area.

The moon had drifted low in the sky by the time they came to a big cemetery near the ocean. It had large statues and big old trees with spiky branches, the kind that looked like they were reaching out to grab someone. Old, worn-down graves dotted the grass as far as Max could see. Glowing green mist seeped out of the ground.

"This is one of the oldest cemeteries in the country," Peter growled. "How could the banshees dare do this here? These graves should be left alone."

Max looked around at the ancient gravestones. All these people had died long before he was born. Then he wondered, since Peter was so old, was it possible he knew some of the people buried there? Maybe that was why it bothered him so much.

"Tim and Lucas," Peter said. "This is a big cemetery, you have to move fast so we don't miss our chance."

They nodded.

"Frank, Kate, try to keep that hill between you and the banshees, so they won't see you until the last moment."

Kate and Frank nodded, too.

"Do you have any questions?" Peter asked.

Max shook his head and growled with the other werewolves. They were all eager to fight.

"Let's do this!" Max said.

TWENTY-THREE

This Means War

THEY SPLIT INTO PAIRS. Tim ran off with Lucas toward the trees. Kate and Frank dashed up the hill together while Becca and Rachel circled back to the gate. Max and Peter stayed in the middle of the cemetery.

"Do you still remember what to do?" Peter asked, bracing his paws and watching the ground.

"Yeah, I got it," Max said turned to face the other way, watching the ground behind Peter with his tail swishing.

He could feel the dirt deep under the ground start to move.

A wolf howled from the top of the hill. Another howl came from the trees. Then the earth cracked in front of Max and bony grey fingers pushed out of the grave in front of him. A dirty arm followed.

Max howled. *AWOOOOOOOooooooooo.*

Then the battle began. Max and Peter fought side by side, tearing apart the zombies in their area of the cemetery. Max heard the others fighting, too. Bones snapped. Brains squished. Old, dry flesh ripped like cracked leather.

Max and Peter worked together. When three zombies tried to grab Peter from behind, Max jumped and crushed them to a pulp beneath his strong paws.

Peter ripped the head off another zombie that tried to bite Max.

"Thanks," Max said and flashed a toothy smile before another zombie appeared. He could attack and think at the same time now. He felt unstoppable.

Then they heard a howl from the other side of the cemetery. Max recognized Tim's voice. Another howl followed quickly after it, Lucas. Peter and Max stopped killing zombies and looked up.

On the far side of the cemetery, the banshees came into view. Their stringy black hair floated around their heads. In the moonlight, their skin seemed to glow. Even over the distance, Max could see the pointed teeth in their blood-red mouths.

Max and Peter raced to that side of the cemetery together.

The banshees floated out over the graves. Around

them, the glowing green mist grew thicker. They must have heard the wolves howling, but they didn't seem to care.

"You take the right!" Peter panted.

"Got it!" Max barked.

They split up and jumped in between the banshees and the trees to cut off their retreat.

Max and Peter snarled, stepping closer to the three floating monsters. Max came up to them from the right and Peter came from the left. Up close, the banshees looked more terrifying than they had from across the graveyard. Like horrible pale ghosts from a nightmare.

According to the plan, Becca and Rachel were supposed to provide backup.

Max craned his neck and let out a breath when he saw them running over from the hill. When they arrived, the girls hung back, waiting for the right time to make their move.

The banshees seemed to finally notice the werewolves. They moved away further into the field. Max and Peter trailed them, but didn't attack yet. They kept their distance and waited. Max hoped they were out of range of the banshees' screams.

Zombies started to crumble out of the ground around them. Their rotten smell made Max's nose crinkle.

Becca and Rachel jumped in to destroy them. They bit and kicked and tore the zombies apart. The girls killed the zombies faster than Max would have believed. With their help, Max and Peter could ignore the zombies and focus on the banshees.

A short bark sounded from the woods. Tim and Lucas were in position.

"That's it. Let's go," Peter said.

Max snarled, ready to fight. They ran at the banshees together. The banshees dodged them and flew away across the field. Max kept on their right while Peter stayed on their left. Max leapt into the air, vaulting off a zombie that was in his way. He laughed when it crashed into another one and fell to the ground. Across from him, Peter bit a zombie's head off without even slowing. They had to keep up with their targets.

When they had almost reached the woods, the banshees sped up and headed for the tree cover.

Peter and Max ran faster, too. They got closer, almost catching them. Then the banshees vanished into the trees.

Max and Peter skidded to a stop at the edge of the woods. There was a horrible snarl, a piercing scream, a shriek. Then the banshees burst out of the trees again.

Lucas and Tim had their teeth in one of them. The

banshee dragged them through the low branches. Tim scraped at her with his claws, trying to get a better grip.

Max jumped in too, clamping down hard on the banshee's arm. The tough flesh was hard to bite into and tasted like dry old leather.

Peter joined them, his added weight dragging the banshee down to the ground. Max pressed his paw down on the banshee's back, tearing at her with his teeth. He felt the others around him, growling and breathing heavily. The banshee thrashed under their claws.

Suddenly, something cracked, and the banshee

crumbled into dust. Everyone was quiet for a moment, too surprised to say anything.

"It worked," Max said.

"I can't believe it," Tim said.

"We got one!" Lucas barked.

They all started laughing in relief and sneezing dust out of their noses.

Then a banshee screamed on the other side of the field. A werewolf howled in pain.

TWENTY-FOUR

Final Showdown

THE SIX WEREWOLVES raced across the cemetery together. When they reached the far side of a low hill, they found their enemies waiting. The two banshees floated low in the mist over the gravestones. Kate and Frank lay on the grass below them, not moving.

"You two, on the right. You two, take the left. Max, you're with me," Peter said.

They split into three groups and closed in on the banshees, drawing them away from the big furry mounds on the ground.

"Fan out!" Peter barked.

The wolves split up. They spread out and made a big circle around the banshees, growling and snarling.

Max looked over at Frank and Kate where they lay

between the rows of gravestones. Frank's silver fur shone in the moonlight. Max thought he could see their bellies moving a little. Were they still breathing? He hoped so.

Lucas was watching them, too. He whined. That was his sister lying there.

Seeing them lying helpless, Max realized how dangerous this fight actually was. He wondered what would happen if his parents found his room empty in the morning. What would they do if he never came home? He tried to swallow his fear.

"Focus! Lucas! Max!" Peter barked.

The banshees turned toward Max and screamed.

Max tried to jump out of the way, but the screams hit him, and he crumpled to the ground in pain.

Lying on the ground, Max couldn't see the fight anymore. His whole body felt broken. The stink of the green mist swirled around his nose, but he couldn't even make himself cough. A moment later the ground cracked next to him and something cold twisted around his leg. It started tugging at him. Max couldn't howl in fear, but he didn't have to wait long before he felt the fur of another wolf beside him, pulling the zombie off.

Max saw Frank, as good as new, jump over him and join in the battle. The white hair on his back bristled. His eyes glowed red. His fangs glistened.

Max's head still pounded with pain, but he forced

himself up into a crouch. The other wolves were growling and snarling somewhere to his right. He turned on shaky legs, looking for the banshees.

The earth cracked under him and he stumbled away from the zombie hand that was pushing out of the ground. His legs collapsed under him and he crumpled to the ground again.

A few minutes later, Max felt well enough to stand. He pushed himself up onto all four paws. His body still hurt, and his mouth tasted of blood. But when one of the others yelped, he shook off the feeling and joined the others in fighting again.

Now all eight wolves were in the fight. The banshees tried to get away, but the werewolves surrounded them on all sides.

The banshees glided right and left, dodging teeth and claws. Then Lucas, Max, and Tim jumped on them at once.

Max got his teeth in one. She was horribly strong. She shook her leg to get him off, but he held on and his weight pulled her down. Becca, Tim, and Rachel jumped on, too. But just when they thought they had her, the other banshee rammed into them. She hit them so hard Max felt some of his ribs snap. He heard the others yelp in pain, too.

They landed hard on the ground. It only took a

couple of seconds for them to get up again. But the banshees were already vanishing in the distance.

Frank and Lucas snarled after them.

Kate turned to Peter. "I'm sorry. I wasn't fast enough. They hit me and Frank before we could dodge out of the way."

Peter was starting to chuckle. "It doesn't matter, Katie."

"But they got away!" Kate said.

"Two of them got away. But we killed one."

Her mouth fell open. "Really?"

"That's right," Becca smiled. "We killed one at the ambush."

"And we'll get the other two," Peter added. "It's only a matter of time."

He looked over at Max and smiled. "Now that we can work as a team."

Max stared into the trees where the banshees had vanished, then looked around at the rest of the pack standing with him.

They hadn't defeated all their enemies yet. But they had survived without much injury. They'd even taken out one of the banshees, something that had never happened before. And they'd learned how to use their desire to protect others to help them control themselves.

Now they were a team, and nothing could stop them for long.

TWENTY-FIVE

Fourth of July

Max sat on a big blanket with his family and sipped on a can of root beer.

The sky around them had already darkened, but the early summer air still felt warm and humid. There were other families on the grassy hillside, too. The whole area was dotted with blankets and chairs.

It was the Fourth of July and everyone was waiting for the fireworks to start over the water.

Ever since the werewolves killed one of the banshees four months ago, the zombie attacks hadn't happened as often. And they hadn't seen the two remaining banshees again at all. It was like they were trying to hide from the werewolves, or maybe they found some other places to haunt.

For the past month, only one or two wolves went out

every night. The rest joined only if they found the glowing green mist. The pack knew that if they found the banshees again, they would destroy them. As Peter had said, It was only a matter of time.

"Girls, stay here. Don't run off!" Max's mom called.

"Mommy, can I go climb the tree?" Maddie asked.

"Not right now, sweetie. You finish your food first, okay?"

Mia grabbed a handful of potato chips and crushed them in her fists. She had chip crumbs in her hair.

Max laughed at her when she stuffed chips in her mouth and growled at him like a monster.

"Now, Mia, let's not do that." Max's dad took the bag of chips away from her and tried to brush the chip crumbs off her head.

"My chips!" Mia whined. She reached for more.

"We don't play with our food," his dad said.

"No! My chips! Mine!" Mia cried.

"Hey, Max!" Tim called as he walked up to their picnic spot.

"Hi, Tim!" Max said, waving from his spot on the blanket.

"Timmy! Did you come to watch the fireworks with us?" Max's dad asked.

"I wanted to ask if Max could come over to our

place. My dad will give him a ride home. We're going to go get ice cream after the fireworks and—"

"I want ice cream!" Maddie jumped up and down.

"Ay-skeem!" Mia squealed, copying her sister.

"You girls didn't even finish your dinner!" Max's mom said.

"Go ahead, Max," his dad said, still trying to get the chips out of Mia's hair.

Max got up and ran off with Tim while his sisters continued whining about ice cream. They wove their way through the blankets and chairs and dodged a couple of kids swinging sparklers around.

"We're not really going to watch the fireworks," Tim said once they were out of earshot. "Peter called. Rachel found some green mist on the other side of the water."

"Does that mean no ice cream either?"

Tim laughed. "There will be if we finish the fight and get back in time. If we're too late, we'll probably just be in trouble."

They ran down the hill and out of sight. When they reached the water, they went wolf, jumped the fence, and started to swim.

Max looked up when the fireworks started to explode in the sky above them. Blue, red, orange, and green lights sparkled and flashed in the night.

When they reached the other side, Tim and Max climbed out onto the rocky shore. Water poured from their dark fur. It splashed into puddles between their paws. They shook, spraying the salty water in a shower all around them.

"Are you two ready?" Peter stepped out from behind a boulder. The rest of the pack waited in the shadows behind him. Their eyes gleamed in the dark.

Max and Tim looked at each other, and then grinned at Peter.

"We're always ready," Tim said.

"Let's go kill some zombies," Max growled.

Back on the grassy hill, Max's mom, dad, and sisters sat on their blanket and watched the fireworks together.

When the booms weren't too loud, Maddie thought she could hear wolves howling somewhere far away in the woods. It was kind of funny. She wondered if wolves liked fireworks, too.

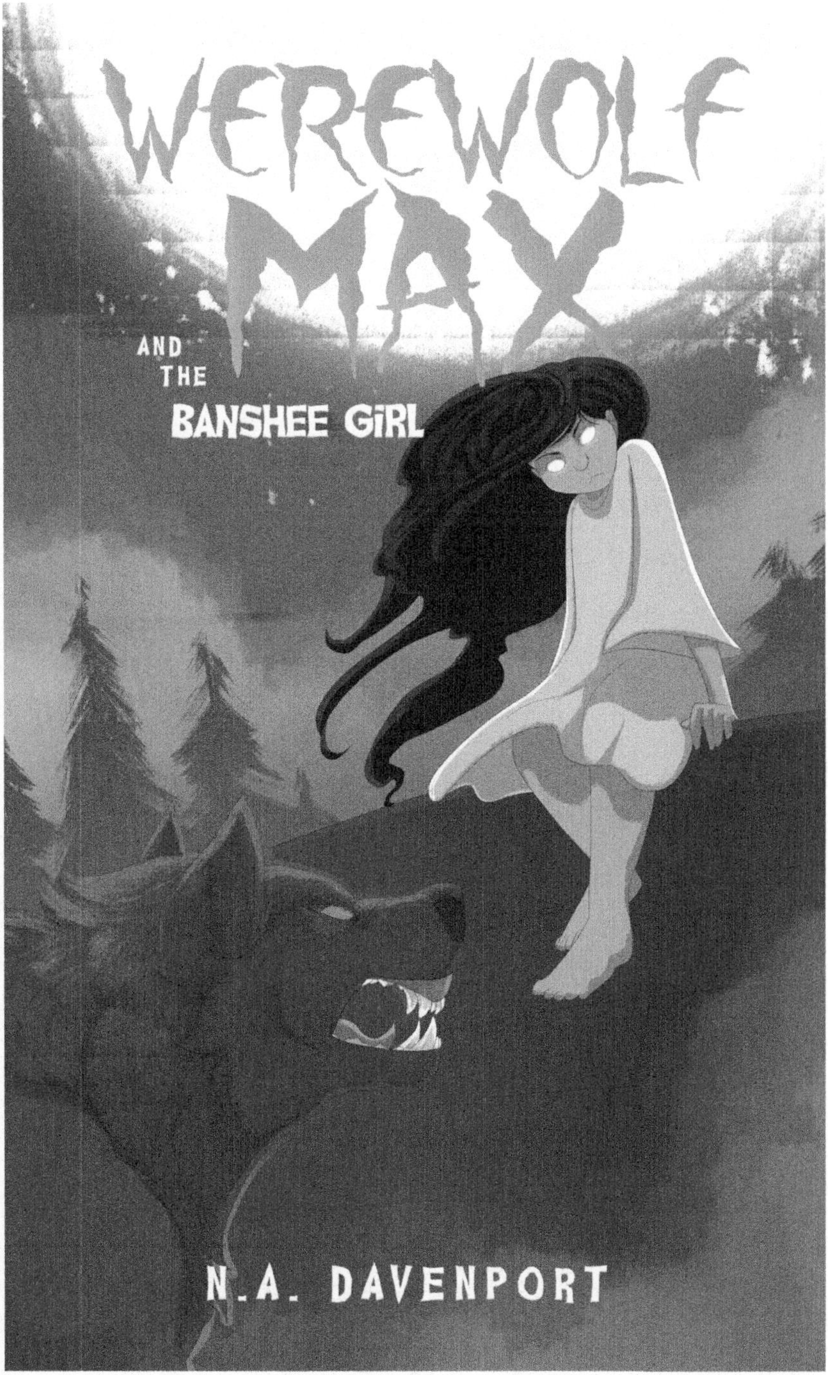
WEREWOLF
MAX
AND
THE
BANSHEE GIRL
N.A. DAVENPORT

Werewolf Max and the Banshee Girl

CHAPTER 1 ON PATROL

"Do you see the mist?" Peter's deep voice sounded tense as they stopped at crest of the hill. His black fur bristled, making him look even bigger than usual.

Max peered down at the old cemetery in the distance. A chilly green mist crept out of the ground among the tombstones, giving the whole place an eerie glow. In the trees around them, dying leaves scratched and scraped against one another with the breeze.

Max flattened his ears and bared his sharp teeth. "The zombies will be there soon," he growled. "Should I call the others?"

"Let's get down there first. We're too near the houses. People might hear us."

"Oh, okay." Max lowered his ears in disappointment.

Without another word, Peter shot down the hill as swiftly and silently as a rush of wind.

Max swished his tail and bolted after him through the cool night air. The two wolves raced through the darkest trees, keeping out of sight of the road, then veered left toward the cemetery.

The stink of the glowing mist drifted toward them, bringing with it the chill of early fall. Max wrinkled his nose at the familiar odor of rotting meat. Together, they leaped over the low stone wall that surrounded the graveyard and skidded to a stop among the tombstones.

Peter eyed the area quickly, then lifted his head to let out a deep, long howl. *AwoooOOOOoooo*

"Hey, I thought *I* was going to call the others!" Max whined.

Peter's glowing red eyes turned to Max. "Why does it matter?"

Max huffed and turned his head away without answering.

He felt annoyed but also a little ashamed at himself. Peter was right, it shouldn't matter who signaled the rest of the pack. The important thing was that they all worked together to protect their town from the zombies. But the older werewolves were always treating him like a kid, never letting him do the important jobs. Sometimes, it felt like they thought he just tagged along for fun.

Hadn't he proven himself? He'd fought in countless zombie battles already. He was one of the werewolves who'd actually killed a banshee. And, most of all, *he* was the one who'd figured out how to go wolf without everyone turning into monsters and fighting each other. Because of Max, they all worked together in battle now. That should count for something, right?

Apparently not. The older wolves still acted like he hung around just to learn from them instead of being a useful member of the pack. Being treated like a baby all the time was starting to get on his nerves.

Peter was still watching him with an annoyingly patient expression on his face. "We're here to destroy zombies, remember?"

"Yeah, yeah, fine." Max rolled his eyes. Of course, he hadn't forgotten.

They trotted out into the graveyard. The smelly mist drifted around them, swirling around the tombstones and making everything look green.

"I wish we knew where the mist came from," Max said, carefully feeling the earth with his paws for any movement underground.

"The banshees make it, you know that." Peter reminded him without looking up.

"Well, yeah, obviously!" Max snorted. "I mean, *how* do they make it? And *why* do they make it, other than to make zombies? Are they trying to take over the world? Do they have to be nearby? If they make mist once, do they have to wait before they can make it again? If we figure them out, maybe it will be easier to fight them."

The banshees were their true enemy. The werewolves searched every night for the green mist and zombies. But they really wanted to find the floating, pale, sharp-fanged banshees with deadly screams. If they got rid of the banshees, there would be no more zombies ever.

Max had helped kill one banshee already. At the time, everyone thought finding and killing the other two would be easy. But it turned out they were wrong. The other two banshees hadn't shown up again all summer and it was starting to get frustrating.

"Listen!" Peter whispered. His ears perked up and he darted away to the other side of the cemetery where the mist was growing thicker.

Max followed him, and then he heard it too. Under the ground, the dirt shifted and crunched.

"The zombies are coming," Max said. In the pale green light with the chilly breeze blowing through his fur, his voice came out more scared than he'd intended. He shook out his fur and cleared his throat.

In the distance, a high piercing howl echoed over the hills. It was followed by another, and then another.

Both Peter and Max lifted their ears.

"Kate, Lucas, and Becca," Max said. Since Max had become a werewolf, nearly eight months earlier, he'd come to recognize the unique voices of all the pack members. It helped to know who was calling and who was on their way in situations like this.

At his side, Peter nodded. "Just in time."

The ground at Max's paws lifted. Roots snapped apart as the soil cracked open.

Max took a step back, wrinkling his nose in disgust. No matter how many zombie battles he'd been in, Max could never get used to the disgusting smell of rotted flesh.

Peter snarled and braced for the attack.

The mound of dirt crumbled away, and a pair of grey arms pushed through, followed by a pale dead face with stringy white hair.

"We'll have to hold them off until the others get here," Peter growled through his teeth.

"Not a problem!" Max said. His fur bristled in anticipation.

More graves were breaking open. Dirty rotting hands and arms clawed their way out, followed by decaying heads and ragged bodies.

Max snarled at the zombies surrounding them. Then Peter leapt forward to attack and Max followed, ripping the closest zombie to pieces with his claws.

Continue the adventure in Werewolf Max and the Banshee Girl, available wherever books are sold.

Made in the USA
Coppell, TX
10 March 2021

51537630R00080